Barn Raising

Craig Brown

Greenwillow Books
An Imprint of HarperCollins Publishers

After the fire there was no place
on Jacob's farm to keep the animals.

A neighbor made space
for them in his barn.

Twice a day Jacob walked to his
neighbor's farm to milk his family's cows.

Friends and neighbors helped Jacob's father clear away the burned barn and lay the foundation for a new one.

On the day of the barn raising,
even before the sun rose over the hills,

people came from all over the county to help.

At first it was hard to tell

what kind of building was going up.

But it wasn't long until the skeleton

of a barn took shape.

The men worked steadily in the hot sun.

They were glad to have cool water.

And when it was time to eat,
the workers set their tool belts down,

removed their hats, and hurried to the
picnic tables to sit in the shade.

Their plates were heaped with chicken, mashed potatoes, vegetables, and date pudding.

After saying grace, the workers dug in.

In the afternoon it was time to start roofing.

The outer walls of the barn, called siding,
were added at the same time as the roof.

The men worked as fast as they could.

The sound of hammers ringing could be heard for miles.

The shadows grew longer.

The new barn was almost finished.

While the last piece of siding was nailed to the barn,

Jacob's father began thanking all those who helped him.

The sun was setting as the family's friends and

neighbors drove away in their wagons and buggies.

That evening Jacob milked his family's cows

in the new barn.

ABOUT BARN RAISINGS

A barn is an important building on any working farm. It provides shelter for livestock and storage for hay and equipment. When a barn owned by a member of the Amish community is destroyed, friends and neighbors join together to help build a new one. This is called a barn raising, and it takes place in a single day.

Of course, a barn raising needs a great deal of preparation. The farmer must clear away his old barn and buy lumber for the new one. He must be sure he has the right equipment for such a big job and it is in good working order. And his wife must get ready to feed all the people who will help build the new barn.

On the day of the barn raising, the workers choose a Head Carpenter from among themselves. Led by the Head Carpenter, the men work together to build wooden frames for the barn. Using ropes to pull and poles to push the frames into place, a skeleton of the barn rises quickly. With only a break for a midday meal, the work progresses steadily, and by evening a new barn rises out of the landscape.

The barn raising on which this book is based took place in Iowa. There are also Amish communities in Pennsylvania, Indiana, Ohio, and northern New York State, and barn raisings, marked by the spirit of hard work and cooperation shown here, might be held in any of them.

To Sharron, for the support and encouragement of the years, and to Sylvia, who taught me the love of art at an early age

Barn Raising
Copyright © 2002 by Craig McFarland Brown
All rights reserved.
Printed in Hong Kong by South China Printing Company (1988) Ltd.
www.harperchildrens.com

Pastels and pen and ink were used for the full-color art.
The text type is Trebuchet MS.

Library of Congress Cataloging-in-Publication Data
Barn raising / by Craig McFarland Brown.
p.   cm.
"Greenwillow Books."
Summary: An Amish community gathers to erect a barn in one day, and
finishes in time for the owner's cows to be milked there that very evening.
ISBN 0-06-029399-3 (trade).   ISBN 0-06-029400-0 (lib. bdg.)
[1. Barns—Fiction. 2. Farm life—Fiction. 3. Amish—Fiction.]
I. Title.   PZ7.B81287 Bar 2002   [E]—dc21   00-063644